Boardsailing

by Phyllis J. Perry

CAPSTONE BOOKS

an imprint of Capstone Press
Mankato, Minnesota

Capstone Books are published by Capstone Press
151 Good Counsel Drive, P.O. Box 669, Mankato, Minnesota 56002
http://www.capstone-press.com

Printed in the United States of America.

Library of Congress Cataloging-in-Publication Data
Perry, Phyllis Jean.
    Boardsailing/by Phyllis J. Perry.
    p. cm.—(Extreme sports)
    Includes bibliographical references (p. 45) and index.
    Summary: Describes the history, equipment, techniques, competition, and safety concerns related to the sport of boardsailing or windsurfing.
    ISBN 0-7368-0481-1
    1. Windsurfing—Juvenile literature. [1. Windsurfing.] I. Title: Boardsailing.
II. Title. III. Series.

GV811.63.W56 P47 2000
797.3'3—dc21   99-053161

Editorial Credits
Carrie A. Braulick, editor; Timothy Halldin, cover designer; Kia Bielke, production designer and illustrator; Heidi Schoof, photo researcher

Photo Credits
Frank S. Balthis, 21
Index Stock Imagery, 4, 43; Index Stock Imagery/Eric Sanford, 10
International Stock/Eric Sanford, cover, 7, 30
James Randklev, 8, 16, 37, 40
Photo Network/Larry Dunmire, 14, 18, 34, 38; Stephen Saks, 29, 32
Photo Resource Hawaii, 22; Tami Dawson/Photo Resource Hawaii, 26
S. Newman Darby, 13

1 2 3 4 5 6 05 04 03 02 01 00

Thank you to Holly Macpherson, United States Windsurfing Association, for her assistance in preparing this book.

Table of Contents

Chapter 1
Boardsailing

Boardsailing is a sport that combines sailing and surfing. Surfers use boards called surfboards to ride on waves. Boardsailors use boards attached to sails to move across water. These are called sailboards. People also call the sport windsurfing or sailboarding.

Many boardsailors compete against one another. Some boardsailors compete in races. Others perform stunts that demand great physical skill.

Wavesailing
Wavesailing is one kind of boardsailing. Wavesailors ride on large waves. They often ride waves in the ocean.

Some boardsailors sail on large waves in the ocean.

Wavesailors sometimes use waves to jump into the air. Wavesailors sail into the steepest part of waves to jump. They then crouch and put their weight on their back foot. The wind then lifts wavesailors into the air.

Wavesailors can jump because they have a sail. These sails use the power of the wind to move the boards across water. Surfers cannot jump because they do not use sails.

Many wavesailors perform stunts. These wavesailors are called freestylers. They sometimes perform stunts in the air. For example, freestylers may do mid-air flips. They also may railride. Freestylers tip their board on its side to perform this trick. They then stand on the board's edge. Some freestylers perform head dips. These freestylers put their head in the water while they sail.

Some places such as Hawaii are known for having large waves. Wavesailors ride waves called swells in many of these places. Wind from storms hundreds of miles or kilometers from the shore often causes swells.

Sails allow wavesailors to jump into the air.

Freestylers ride on the edge of their boards to perform railrides.

These waves have long, continuous crests. Some boardsailors wavesail in water off the coast of Australia or the Canary Islands. These islands are located off the western coast of Africa. Boardsailors also wavesail near islands in the Caribbean Sea.

Racing

Many boardsailors compete in races. Some boardsailors race on large waves as wavesailors do. But others race on lakes or other bodies of water with small waves.

Different styles of boardsail racing exist. Some races are one-design competitions. All racers use the same sailboards in these races. Other competitions are open-class races. Boardsailors can use different brands and types of boards in these races. They can change their equipment to help them sail at faster speeds. For example, they may use different sails. Racers in one-design competitions cannot change their equipment.

Many boardsailors race on triangular courses. These courses are in the shape of a triangle. Triangular courses sometimes are called Olympic courses. Boardsailors in the Olympic Games race on triangular courses.

Chapter 2
History

It is not known who invented sailboards. Some people believe an English boy named Peter Chilvers invented the first sailboard in 1958. Others believe S. Newman Darby invented the first sailboard. He wrote the first description of a sailboard design. It appeared in the August 1965 issue of *Popular Science* magazine.

Darby's first boards were made of wood. Darby built the sailboards in a rectangular shape and attached a sail. Darby and his brother Ken made about 160 sailboards by 1966. They sold the boards in their store.

Some early sailboards were made of wood. Today's sailboards are made of lighter materials.

The Windsurfer

Hoyle Schweitzer and Jim Drake invented the first popular sailboard design in 1965. Schweitzer was a businessman and a surfer. Drake was an engineer and a sailor. Schweitzer and Drake's boards were made of plastic. They measured 12 feet (3.7 meters) long. They had long, slim bodies with flat bottoms. Booms supported the sails. These bars go across the bottom of sails on both sides. Boardsailors use booms to steer. Schweitzer and Drake's board became known as a Windsurfer. The inventors started a company called the Windsurfer Company to make the boards.

The Windsurfer Company improved its designs over the next several years. By 1970, the company made Windsurfers from plastic coated with fiberglass. This strong, light material is made of woven glass fibers. These sailboards were lighter and easier to handle than the earlier boards. In 1978, Windsurfers included two footstraps. These helped boardsailors stay on their boards in strong winds.

S. Newman Darby's first boards were rectangular.

Boardsailing in Europe

In the early 1970s, people in Europe became interested in boardsailing. The sport was especially popular in Germany. Many Europeans enjoyed downhill skiing during winter. They boardsailed during summer to stay in shape. About 150,000 sailboards were sold in Europe between 1973 and 1978.

Boardsailing is a very popular sport throughout the world.

Some European companies began to make sailboards. In the early 1970s, a manufacturing company in the Netherlands named Ten Cate began producing sailboards. In 1975, the Windglider Company of Germany started making sailboards. In 1976, the

Mistral Company of Switzerland began making sailboards.

Boardsailing's Popularity Grows

Boardsailing soon became popular in other parts of the world. The sport became popular in North America in the late 1970s. In 1984, boardsailing was included in the Summer Olympic Games in Los Angeles.

Today, boardsailing continues to be a popular sport. More than 100 sailboard companies exist today. Professional racing events became common in the early 1990s. Professional boardsailors earn cash prizes for winning competitions.

Chapter 3
Equipment and Safety

Boardsailors should pay attention to safety. They use the proper equipment. They boardsail only in good weather conditions. Boardsailors also are respectful to other boardsailors. They may let other boardsailors go ahead of them in crowded boardsailing areas. This helps boardsailors avoid crashes.

Rigging Up Boards

Boardsailors need to know how to rig up their sailboards before they get on the water. This helps prevent equipment problems as they sail. A sailboard's rig includes a sail, mast, and booms.

Boardsailors use the proper equipment to help keep them safe.

Boardsailors insert and secure the mast. This long pole fits into a sleeve in the sail. Masts support sails in the wind.

Some boardsailors use boards with a daggerboard. This narrow piece of plastic extends from underneath the board. Boardsailors fit daggerboards into a slot in their boards. Daggerboards prevent boards from slipping sideways. They sometimes are called centerboards.

Boardsailors may only use daggerboards in certain wind conditions. They usually use boards with daggerboards in light or moderate winds. Most boardsailors use boards without daggerboards in strong winds of about 12 knots. A knot is a measurement of speed across water. It is equal to about 1.15 miles (2 kilometers) per hour.

Sailboards
Sailboards have some basic features. Many are made from plastic or fiberglass. The top of the boards have a non-skid surface. This helps

Boardsailors must know how to rig up their boards before they go on the water.

prevent boardsailors from slipping off their boards.

Boardsailors may use long or short boards. Long boards usually are about 12 feet (4 meters) long and 2.5 feet (1 meter) wide. Boardsailors often use long boards in light winds. Most long boards have daggerboards. Beginners often use long boards. These boards are more stable and easier to control than short boards.

Wavesailors often use short boards. These boards sometimes are called funboards. Short boards are easier to control in strong winds. Most short boards do not have daggerboards. Short boards have footstraps to help boardsailors balance and steer.

Boardsailors divide boards into groups according to their buoyancy. They judge how well the boards float. These groups include floaters and sinkers. Floaters usually float better than sinkers. But a board's buoyancy depends on the boardsailor's weight. Heavier boardsailors make boards sink more than lighter boardsailors.

Sails come in different sizes.

Sails

Sails come in different types and sizes.
More than 1,000 different types of sails are
available. Sails are measured in square meters.
Sails range in size from 2 square meters (22
square feet) to larger than 10 square meters
(110 square feet). Most sails have a window
made of clear film. This allows boardsailors
to see through their sails.

Boardsailors use booms to steer their boards.

Boardsailors use different types of sails in different wind conditions. They use small sails in strong winds. They use large sails in light winds. Many boardsailors use sails between 5 square meters (54 square feet) and 8 square meters (86 square feet) in size. Heavier boardsailors may choose to use larger sails. These sails provide more power to push boardsailors through the water.

Some sails are designed for a certain type of boardsailing. For example, wavesailors use wave sails. These sails have less material at the bottom than most other sails. This allows wavesailors to perform stunts more easily.

Masts, Booms, and Harnesses

Masts are made of different materials and come in different sizes. Most masts are made of fiberglass or carbon fiber. Carbon fiber is a strong, light material made of fibers. Masts are about 13 to 16 feet (4 to 5 meters) long. Some masts come in two pieces. These masts are easier to store than masts that are only one piece.

Booms may be round or oval. Boardsailors use booms to steer and control their boards. They also use booms to keep their balance. Some booms are made of aluminum. Others are made of carbon fiber. Booms have a soft rubber grip to help make booms more comfortable to hold.

Boardsailors usually wear a harness in strong winds. These pieces of padded nylon webbing connect boardsailors to their booms. Boardsailors may use seat, waist, or chest harnesses. The style boardsailors choose depends on their type of boardsailing. Harnesses have a front hook. Boardsailors use two ropes to attach the booms to the loop on their harnesses. These ropes usually are made of polyester covered with waterproof material.

Harnesses help boardsailors support their rigs in strong winds. They lessen strain on boardsailors' backs. Boardsailors usually do not need harnesses in light winds.

Judging Weather Conditions

Safe boardsailors learn how to tell if weather conditions are favorable for boardsailing. They pay special attention to wind conditions. Boardsailors learn to correctly judge wind speed. They do not boardsail in storms or in conditions that are too difficult for them to handle.

Some boardsailors use the Beaufort scale to help them judge wind speed. This scale uses numbers to show wind force. It includes the wind speed in miles and kilometers per

Beaufort Scale of Wind Speed

	Wind	(km/h)	(mph)	Visual Observations
0	Calm	0	0	Smoke rises upward
1	Light air	1–5	1–3	Wind direction given by smoke but not by wind vane
2	Light breeze	6–11	4–7	Leaves rustle; wind vane moves; can feel wind on the face
3	Gentle breeze	12–19	8–12	Leaves are in constant motion
4	Moderate breeze	20–29	13–18	Small branches move; dust and loose paper lift
5	Fresh breeze	30–39	19–24	Small trees with leaves sway; wavelets form on inland waters
6	Strong breeze	40–50	25–31	Large branches move; utility lines seem to whistle
7	Near gale	51–61	32–38	Whole trees move; somewhat difficult to walk into the wind
8	Gale	62–74	39–46	Twigs break off trees; difficult to walk into the wind
9	Strong gale	75–87	47–54	Slight damage to buildings
10	Storm	88–102	55–63	Trees uprooted; considerable damage to buildings
11	Violent storm	103–119	64–74	Widespread damage
12	Hurricane	120+	75+	Extreme destruction of property

hour. The scale also lists visual signs boardsailors can use to judge the wind's speed.

Other Safety Practices

Boardsailors keep themselves safe in other ways. They should be good swimmers. It also is helpful for boardsailors to know basic lifesaving skills. Boardsailors often sail with others. Other boardsailors can help if they fall off their boards or have trouble in the water.

Boardsailors who have trouble stay with their boards. They do not swim for shore. They remove their rigs from their boards and fold up the sails. Boardsailors secure their rigs to their boards. They then kneel or lie down on the boards and paddle to shore.

Beginning boardsailors learn basic skills before they try advanced skills. Beginners who try boardsailing in strong winds may hurt themselves. Some beginning boardsailors tie their boards to an object on shore. This keeps their boards in one spot in the water. These boardsailors then can practice balancing on their boards. Some

Some beginning boardsailors practice on land.

beginners even practice on dry land before they enter the water. Beginning boardsailors usually ride their boards in light winds. They sometimes go to boardsailing schools to learn basic boardsailing skills.

Safe boardsailors follow other safety measures. They take breaks when they become tired. Boardsailors who are tired may put themselves or others in danger. Boardsailors check all of their equipment before and after they sail. They make sure it is in good condition.

Safety Equipment

Boardsailors use safety equipment. Sailboards have a universal joint. This shaft keeps the sail attached to the board. A strong strap goes around the joint. This strap holds the board and sail together if the universal joint breaks. Boardsailors who sail in very strong winds may wear safety helmets. Helmets protect boardsailors' heads if they fall off their boards.

Boardsailors may wear helmets and wet suits.

Boardsailors should wear wet suits in cold water. These rubber, waterproof suits fit closely to boardsailors' bodies. Wet suits help prevent boardsailors from getting hypothermia. This condition occurs when a person's body temperature becomes too low.

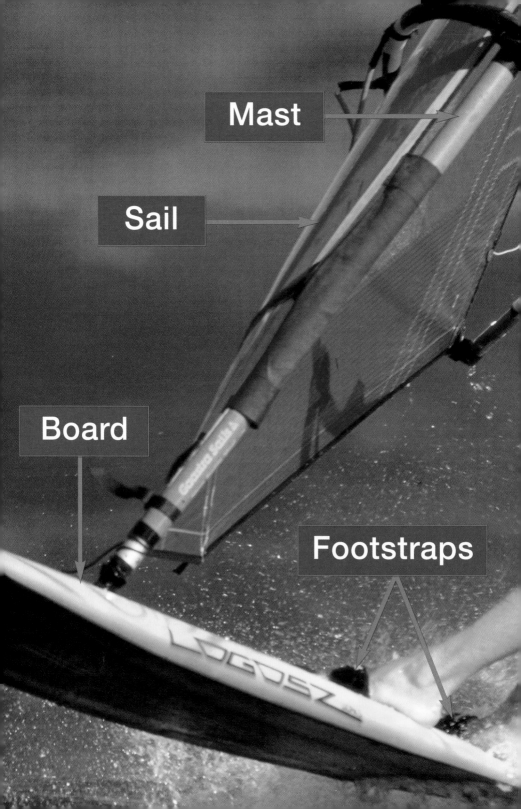

Boom

Wet Suit

Harness

Chapter 4

Skills

Boardsailors need a variety of skills and abilities. They should be good swimmers. Boardsailors also need good balance to stay on their boards. They use footwork to control and steer their boards.

Footwork

Boardsailors use their feet to control their boards. They often change the position of their feet. Boardsailors may place their feet close together or leave more space between them. Adjusting their feet helps them make turns and keep their boards steady.

Boardsailors use their feet to help them control their boards.

Boardsailors also vary the amount of weight they place on their feet. They may push down with one foot to speed up a turn. They also may put more pressure on one foot to keep their boards steady in strong winds.

Controlling Sailboards

Boardsailors must master many skills to control their boards. They move their booms to steer. They may need to tack. Boardsailors make upwind turns when they tack. They also may need to jibe. Boardsailors make downwind turns when they jibe.

Boardsailors sometimes sail in strong winds. These winds may be more than 15 knots. Boardsailors sometimes lean away from the sail in strong winds. They then may stretch their arms out. This helps boardsailors control their boards.

Boardsailors sometimes lean back and stretch their arms out in strong winds.

Wavesailing Skills

Wavesailors should have advanced boardsailing skills. They also need good judgment and timing.

Wavesailors perform different stunts. They may jump waves. They may glide down the side of waves. They may do forward or backward loops. Wavesailors do these flips in mid-air. Wavesailors also may spin in circles or do donkey kicks. They kick their boards out sideways at the top of jumps to perform donkey kicks.

Many wavesailors perform stunts in the air.

Chapter 5
Competition

Some boardsailors ride their boards for fun.
But many boardsailors compete against each
other. Some boardsailors race in competitions.
They may participate in large races such as the
World Windsurfing Championships or the Pan
American Games. Some boardsailors also race in
the Olympic Games.

Other boardsailors compete in freestyle
competitions. Some of these competitions are part
of the U.S. National Wave Sailing Championship
Tour. The United States Windsurfing Association
(USWA) oversees this annual series of
competitions. Some competitions in this tour

Boardsailors often compete against each other in races.

Slalom racers travel downwind on zigzag courses.

take place in Hawaii. Others take place in the
Atlantic and Pacific Oceans off coasts of the
United States.

Competitive boardsailors may be professionals
or amateurs. Amateur boardsailors usually do not
compete for cash prizes as professionals do.

Professional boardsailors sometimes have
sponsors. These sponsors usually are large
companies that sell sailboards or boardsailing
products. Boardsailors may display their

sponsors' names or logos on their clothing or equipment. Boardsailors also may use their sponsors' equipment. In return, sponsors pay for some of boardsailors' travel expenses, entry fees, or equipment costs.

Course Races

The International Sailing Federation (ISF) governs most course races. This group sets worldwide rules for the sport of sailing. Boardsailors often sail on triangular courses in these races. The courses usually are about 4 miles (6 kilometers) long. Competitors may be divided into groups according to their weight, sex, or age. Course races include one-design and open-class races.

Boardsailors sometimes race on long-distance courses. These courses are at least 12 miles (19 kilometers) long.

Course race competitions may last several days. Boardsailors may race more than 10 times during these competitions. Competitors receive points according to their finishing place in each race. The boardsailor with the lowest point total usually wins the competition.

Other Types of Races

Boardsailors compete in other types of races. They may compete in slalom races. Slalom racers travel downwind through short courses. They race around markers set up in a zigzag pattern. Slalom racers jibe as they race.

Other boardsailors speedsail. These boardsailors sail as fast as possible in very strong winds. Speedsailors may reach speeds of more than 50 miles (80 kilometers) per hour. These boardsailors race in a straight line.

Freestyle Competitions

The first freestyle competition took place off the New York coast in 1975. Today, many boardsailors compete in freestyle competitions. Freestylers plan routines. They then perform these sets of stunts in front of judges. They usually have about three minutes to perform their routines.

Judges watch freestylers from the shore. They award points to freestylers according to the number and difficulty of the stunts. Judges also consider how well freestylers perform

Freestylers receive points based on the number, difficulty, and performance of their stunts.

their stunts. More than 150 freestyle stunts exist in international competitions.

Most boardsailors who compete have advanced boardsailing skills. They work to improve these skills for competitions. Boardsailors will continue to make new challenges for themselves in the future.

Words to Know

booms (BOOMS)—a pair of lightweight, curved bars joined together at both ends of a sail; boardsailors use booms to steer.

daggerboard (DAYG-ur-bord)—a narrow piece of plastic that fits through a slot in a sailboard; daggerboards prevent sailboards from slipping sideways.

freestyle (FREE-stile)—to perform stunts with a sailboard

hypothermia (hye-puh-THUR-mee-uh)—a condition that occurs when a person's body temperature becomes too low

mast (MAST)—a fiberglass or carbon fiber pole that fits into a sail's sleeve; masts support sails in the wind.

rig (RIG)—the sail, mast, and booms of a sailboard

swell (SWEL)—a large wave with a long, continuous crest

To Learn More

Barker, Amanda. *Windsurfing.* Radical Sports. Des Plaines, Ill.: Heinemann Library, 1999.

Bundey, Nikki. *In the Water.* First Sports Science. Minneapolis: Carolrhoda Books, 1998.

Evans, Jeremy. *Windsurfing.* New York: Crestwood House, 1992.

Holden, Phil. *Wind and Surf.* All Action. Minneapolis: Lerner Publications, 1992.

You can read more about boardsailing in *American WindSurfer, Windsurfing,* and *Windsport* magazines.

Useful Addresses

Canadian Yachting Association
1600 James Naismith Drive
Suite 504
Gloucester, ON K1B 5N4
Canada

International Windsurfer Class Association
1955 West 190th Street
Torrence, CA 90509

United States Windsurfing Association
P.O. Box 978
Hood River, OR 97031

Internet Sites

Canadian Yachting Association
http://www.sailing.ca

Sail-USA
http://www.sailusa.com

San Francisco Boardsailing Association
http://www.sfba.org

United States Windsurfing Association
http://www.uswindsurfing.org

Index